THE
BRAVE
BEAR

NICK BLAND

Scholastic Canada Ltd.
Toronto New York London Auckland Sydney
Mexico City New Delhi Hong Kong Buenos Aires

For Dusty

Scholastic Canada Ltd.
604 King Street West, Toronto, Ontario M5V 1E1, Canada

Scholastic Inc.
557 Broadway, New York, NY 10012, USA

Scholastic Australia Pty Limited
PO Box 579, Gosford, NSW 2250, Australia

Scholastic New Zealand Limited
Private Bag 94407, Botany, Manukau 2163, New Zealand

Scholastic Children's Books
Euston House, 24 Eversholt Street, London NW1 1DB, UK

www.scholastic.ca

Library and Archives Canada Cataloguing in Publication

Bland, Nick, 1973-, author, illustrator
The very brave bear / Nick Bland.

Previously published: 2014.
ISBN 978-1-4431-6313-2 (softcover)

I. Title.

PZ10.3.B527Veb 2018   j823'.92   C2017-904028-6

Copyright © 2014 by Nick Bland.
First published by Scholastic Australia in 2014.
This edition published in Canada by Scholastic Canada Ltd. in 2018.
All rights reserved.

5 4 3 2 1   Printed in China 38   18 19 20 21 22

In the Jingle Jangle Jungle
on the edge of Slimy Bog,
Bear was picking berries
from a very wobbly log.

"**AHOY!**" said Boris Buffalo,
from underneath the mud,

and Bear fell off his wobbly log
and landed with a . . .

THUD.

"I didn't mean to scare you,"
said Boris with a grin,
"I only came to ask you if
you wanted to come in."

"I wasn't even scared," said Bear,
"I'm just as brave as you.
The bravest thing that you can do,
I can do it too."

So he balanced like a butterfly
upon the wobbly log.
He did a double somersault . . .

and **SPLASHED**

in Slimy Bog.

"If you're so brave," continued Bear,
"then come and follow me.
We'll see how brave a buffalo is
when climbing up a tree."

So Bear climbed up a mighty tree,
the tallest he could find,
and there was Boris Buffalo,
climbing right behind.

"That was easy!" Boris said,
"And what a pleasant view.
But I can think of something else
that you'd be scared to do."

Boris wandered up a hill,
the steepest he could find,
then tumbled down the other side
. . . and Bear was right behind.

"That was easy!" boasted Bear,
"I'm just as brave as you.
But I can think of something else
that you'd be scared to do."

They crossed a raging river

and they swung between the trees.

They tried to catch a porcupine,

and wear a beard of bees.

Bear and Boris Buffalo were
the bravest of the brave,
until, that is, they came across . . .

A VERY SCARY CAVE!

"It's awfully dark inside," said Boris.
"It's quiet too," said Bear.
Then with his softest voice he said,
"Is anybody there?"

"Maybe we should wait," said Boris,
"until we know for sure."
And then, from in the cave,
there came a very scary . . .

"ROAAAAR!"

Bear and Boris Buffalo had
never been so scared.
They decided not to go inside,
neither of them dared!

They hurried through the jungle
and they hid in Slimy Bog.
And then, from in the cave,
there came . . .

...a **TINY** little frog.

"I didn't mean to scare you,"
said Froggy with a grin,
"I only came to ask you
if you wanted to come in."

So Bear and Boris Buffalo
went back to Froggy's cave,
and agreed that bears and buffaloes . . .

. . . are equally as brave.